A Lady, A Kiss, A Christmas Wish

Daughters of Desire (Scandalous Ladies)
Book One

COLLETTE CAMERON

Blue Rose Romance®

Sweet-to-Spicy Timeless Romance®

A Lady, A Kiss, A Christmas Wish
Copyright © 2020 Collette Cameron®
Cover Art: Jaycee DeLorenzo - Sweet 'N Spicy Designs

Attn: Permissions Coordinator
Blue Rose Romance®
P.O. Box 167, Scappoose, OR 97056

Print Book ISBN: 9781954307032
collettecameron.com

Other Collette Cameron Books

Daughters of Desire (Scandalous Ladies)
A Lady, A Kiss, A Christmas Wish
No Lady for the Lord
Love Lessons for a Lady
His One and Only Lady

Check out Collette's Other Series
Highland Heather Romancing a Scot
The Blue Rose Regency Romances:
The Culpepper Misses
Seductive Scoundrels
The Honorable Rogues®
Heart of a Scot
Castle Brides

Collections
Lords in Love
Heart of a Scot Books 1-3
The Honorable Rogues® Books 1-3
The Honorable Rogues® Books 4-6
Seductive Scoundrels Series Books 1-3
Seductive Scoundrels Series Books 4-6
The Blue Rose Regency Romances-
The Culpepper Misses Series 1-2

Dedication

For the exceptional ladies in my VIP reader group, Collette's Chèris, who helped me name Lady Persephone Poppington and Sir Galahad Whiskerton. I believe they might be the most pampered, fussed over, and adored pets to ever grace the pages of one of my historical romances.

Lora Patten, Lynn Quinlan, Marissa Birch, and Sharon Gilbert Fournier—thank you for your creative suggestions!

Merry Christmas to all of my dear readers!

1

Rochester, England

9 December 1817

Early afternoon

"Miss Winterborne?"

Mrs. Sabella Thackpenny's sleep-thickened, warbly voice yanked Joy from her pleasant daydream about where she'd spend her half-day off this Saturday.

Walking in The Vines Gardens?

Browsing the shelves at Barclay's Book Shoppe and Emporium?

Or—the thought nearly made her sigh aloud in anticipation—perhaps enjoying a cup of *strong,* sweet tea with milk at that quaint tea shop on High Street where she and her friend Mercy Feathers had enjoyed maid of honor tarts two years ago?

Mercy was the governess for two young charges here in Rochester.

Had it truly been two years since Joy had seen her friend?

Lips pressed tight, she shook her head the slightest bit.

It didn't seem possible that much time had passed.

She clearly remembered the Christmas decorations and gingerbread cookies that day. She could still almost smell the evergreens and the cinnamon, cloves, and ginger. Aromas she'd not enjoyed the pleasure of since.

Joy missed the other young women from

Haven House and Academy for the Enrichment of Young Women who had become her sisters in every way except for by blood. She especially missed Mercy, Chasity Nobel, and Purity Mayfield. The four of them had shared a room at the academy for as long as Joy could remember.

All of the cast-off girls who'd ever called Haven House and Academy for the Enrichment of Young Women their home had shared a middle name too. Shepard. The name was a slightly altered version of the kindly but strict and extremely pious Hester Shepherd's own surname.

That sweet, Godly woman had bestowed a Biblical given name upon each discarded child in her loving care. Mrs. Shepherd, now a spinster in her sixth decade, vowed she adored the girls she'd raised since infancy like her own daughters.

The honorary *missus* before her last name was a matter of formality. No proper instructor was ever addressed as a *miss*.

As Mrs. Shepherd had been taking in unwanted charges—all by-blows in one form or another of the wealthy or aristocracy—for two-and-one-half decades, she'd been a mother to nearly seventy girls. All of which she'd raised to be prayerful, moral young women despite their unfortunate beginnings.

"Each of you are a gift from our Lord. He has a purpose in everything. 'All things work together for good to those who love God,'" Mrs. Shepherd quoted to her girls from the scriptures. "Even your presence at Haven House and Academy for the Enrichment of Young Women is no accident. Never forget it, my dears," she admonished fondly.

What was more, Mrs. Shepherd and her discreet staff had provided every girl with an education and skills for respectable employment. Not, however, entirely out of benevolence. Haven House and Academy for the Enrichment of

Young Women and Mrs. Shepherd had been well-compensated for her discretion and the girls' decorous upbringing.

Joy was eternally grateful. She missed the headmistress's light-hearted scolds and contagious laughter. Naturally, they corresponded—quite regularly as a matter of fact. But a piece of paper slashed with tiny, neat script was no substitute for one of Mrs. Shepherd's soft, comforting rose and violet scented hugs.

How very different was the plump, genial headmistress compared to the pinch-faced woman across the room blinking sleepily behind her spectacles, her mouth pursed in a perpetual grimace of disapproval.

Or perhaps Mrs. Thackpenny's turned down mouth was a result of her recent propensity to pass gas with the offensive regularity and unfortunate exuberance of a barnyard animal. A *large* barnyard animal.

Joy held her breath, hoping her employer would settle back into her nap, which was her habit in the afternoon. She longed to return to her daydream about delicious tea and sweet cakes in a cozy teashop. If she couldn't actually consume the treats, at least Joy could fantasize about doing so.

A slight nasally snore resonated from the afghan covered lump, and tension eased from Joy's spine and shoulders. A few more minutes of peace was a treasured blessing.

Mrs. Thackpenny—*pinchpenny is more apt*—only permitted Joy used tea leaves. Leaves which the difficult widow had already used twice herself. The resulting brew was slightly bronze-tinted water, which scarcely tasted of tea at all.

And no sugar or milk. Ever.

"A body can never economize too much, Miss Winterborne," the rail-thin woman had intoned when she'd first retained Joy as her lady's companion. "You'll learn soon enough that

though I'm extremely frugal, I'm not miserly."

Only tightfisted and parsimonious.

"Save a penny, save a pound." As was her wont, Mrs. Thackpenny emphasized the latter colloquialism with a resounding thump of her worse-for-wear cane.

Wasn't the phrase, *A penny saved is a penny earned,* anyway? Or was it, *Look after pennies, and the pounds will look after themselves?*

It didn't matter. What did, however, was Mrs. Thackpenny's tightfistedness.

Persuading the woman to part with funds was as difficult as convincing a nun to toss up her habit for a dockside tumble with a salty sea dog— in broad daylight.

Every single month since her arrival, Joy had been obliged to ask for her allowance and carefully count each coin. For her penny-pinching employer had tried to cheat her out of a shilling or two several times.

Honestly, there wasn't any need for her excessive thrift either.

Mrs. Thackpenny's husband, a successful banker, had left her a considerable fortune. Yet the decades-old worn and quite threadbare carpets, draperies, and outdated furnishings remained as a tribute to the long-dead Mr. Ephraim Thackpenny.

The widow owned precisely seven gowns— one for each day of the week. Every one entirely black from collar to hem and as plain as unused paper, without so much as a shiny button to break the bleak monotony.

Head canted, Joy listened for her employer's drowsy murmurings, and when no more sounds came from the woman, decided Mrs. Thackpenny had, indeed, been mumbling in her sleep. A common enough occurrence, in truth.

Joy happily turned her musings toward her half-day off once more.

Mayhap, she'd indulge in all three activities this Saturday.

The merest rebellious smile bent her mouth

Yes, that was precisely what she'd do.

Visit The Vines, the bookstore, *and* the tea shop.

Pure heaven.

A small frown pulled her eyebrows together as she inserted the needle into the fine linen fabric, another handkerchief for her mistress—Mrs. Thackpenny's one indulgence besides her pampered pets.

That was her plan *if* Mrs. Thackpenny actually permitted Joy the half-day she'd been assured of each week when hired by the difficult woman four years ago—no five years next week. There'd also been promises of exciting trips to Bath, the Continent, routs, musicals, soirees, the theater…museums.

None of which had ever manifested. If Joy

managed a single, short walk outdoors every week, she counted herself most fortunate.

An unintended sigh slipped past her lips.

All fabrications to entice a young girl with stars in her eyes and dreams of a different, more exciting life clouding her common sense.

Little had Joy known that she was the latest in a long queue of lady's maids retained and dismissed since Mrs. Sabella Thackpenny had taken a fall a decade before. Hence the need for her cane, and upon the advice of her then physician, Doctor Daggat, she'd conceded the need for a live-in companion.

Companion was a generous term for what Joy was to the woman. She was expected to be on hand for whatever the difficult widow demanded every hour of every day and night.

In truth, Mrs. Thackpenny seldom allowed Joy her half-day and never compensated for the deliberate oversight.

How Joy craved a few hours of desperately needed reprieve from the demanding, cantankerous, never satisfied woman's presence. There was never a word of thanks or appreciation. Just scolds, complaints, reprimands, and the occasional threat of dismissal.

And dash it to ribbons, that was what Joy could look forward to until Mrs. Thackpenny departed this earth, unless she was somehow able to procure another position. With considerable effort, Joy quashed the wave of frustration billowing up from her middle that her errant, uncharitable thoughts brought on.

She closed her eyes and sent up a silent prayer.

Lord, give me the strength and patience I need. Keep me from complaining and help me be grateful. My life could be so much worse.

Her eyes drifted open.

It could be better too.

But, *this* was her lot in life, and she ought to be appreciative. In truth and much to her astonishment, despite her employer's contentious nature, Joy had grown fond of the impossible woman.

At least she held a position, albeit one that paid poorly and consumed all of her waking hours. But a roof over one's head and food in one's belly, even if the fare was bland and unappetizing, accounted for much. That was more than most young women born on the wrong side of the blanket could say or even hope for.

Of course, Mrs. Thackpenny didn't know that particular scandalous detail about Joy's paternity.

Nor would she ever. The very notion made her ill.

A shiver skittered the length of her spine.

For God help her, Joy's position and reputation depended upon that scandal remaining a secret. As did Haven House and Academy for the Enrichment of Young Women's, and the many girls who had ever called the place home.

Mrs. Shepherd made absolutely certain her *girls'* unsavory origins were diligently guarded and hidden. She created respectable faux backgrounds and prepared them for various positions appropriate for gently-bred young ladies.

She was paid handsomely—*very* handsomely—for her exclusive, confidential services too. Surely she'd amassed enough savings to retire in comfort, yet Mrs. Shepherd cheerfully continued in her position.

It struck Joy as peculiar that a parent who was so eager to hide their by-blow or bastard daughter would pay Mrs. Shepherd's exorbitant fee and ensure their illegitimate offspring had a decent future. But then again, there was no understanding the peculiarities of the wealthy or the peerage, in Joy's limited experience.

Odder still were the surnames Mrs. Shepherd

dubbed each of her charges with. She vowed the name contained a hint about each girl's familial heritage. Nonetheless, to Joy's knowledge, thus far, not a single former ward had identified either parent.

What difference would it make anyway?

"Miss Winterborne?"

Mrs. Thackpenny's voice pitched higher, and the unfortunate wooden floor—already scarred and scraped—received a pair of undeserved petulant thwacks from her ever-present cane.

Thump. Thump.

"*Where* is my darling Sir Galahad Whiskerton?"

Thump. Thump.

"Miss Win-ter-borne? Are you there?"

Her shrill voice pierced the air once more.

Joy winced as she accidentally pricked her finger.

As if she couldn't hear her crotchety

employer's strident tones from the chair less than ten feet away. Rather astonishing that a woman so shrunken and petite could produce such remarkable volume with her reedy voice.

"Yes, Mrs. Thackpenny. Permit me to finish this French knot, please."

Accustomed to her employer's ill-temper, Joy calmly finished her embroidery stitch despite her cold fingers' stiffness.

From beneath her lashes, she cast a yearning glance toward the few insufficient glowing coals in the grate, in front of which Mrs. Thackpenny's small settee was positioned to absorb the stingy warmth the pathetic fire provided.

Was it a sin to covet a smidgen of the sparse warmth for herself?

Little heat radiated past the settee, leaving the rest of the room so frigid, Joy could see her own puffs of breath. She deliberately blew out several, watching the vapor disappear, just to prove her point. Besides the kitchen, this was the warmest room in the house, which wasn't saying much.

The temperature indoors accounted for the two pairs of stockings she wore as well as the housecoat and hand-knitted woolen shawl wrapped around her shoulders and pinned neatly at her bosom with a simple, but elegant silver cross brooch—a parting gift from Mrs. Shepherd. Joy wore fingerless gloves, also hand-knitted, but that didn't prevent the digits from becoming distressingly cold.

As always, because Mrs. Thackpenny preferred a tomb-like atmosphere, the faded burgundy brocade draperies remained closed against the day's chill. Truth be told, Joy would've welcomed meager sunlight streaming through the floor to ceiling arched windows. She couldn't help but think Mrs. Thackpenny would also benefit from a spot of sun.

It couldn't be good for a soul to be shut up

indoors with no light or fresh air for weeks on end. God only knew Joy felt the effects of such confinement. Humans weren't meant to huddle in the dark like frightened insects or creep about in the gloom like earthworms or moles.

"You know I cannot bear for Whiskers to be away from me," the elderly woman complained in a child's sulky voice—a strident voice which grated along Joy's spine like sharp talons scraping the bones.

She's old and lonely, Joy reminded herself. *Be charitable.*

Her husband died when she was not much older than you.

She has no children or remaining family and few friends.

In an attempt to harness her vexation, Joy recited one of the many scriptures Mrs. Shepherd had drilled into her and the other girls.

A kind word turns away wrath.

Kindness had never worked with Mrs. Thackpenny before.

Determined to harness her unkind thoughts, Joy repeated the verse twice more.

A kind word turns away wrath.

A kind word turns away wrath.

Screwing her face into a grimace, she released a noiseless snort.

Pshaw.

Such exercises were useless. Joy would never completely master her thoughts when it came to Mrs. Thackpenny.

The widow could vex the most pious of priests, and Joy had never claimed the benevolence or compassion of a man of the cloth. Nevertheless, with a determined set of her chin and after a deep breath to regain her equanimity, Joy said, "Indeed, I do understand how precious Sir Whiskerton and Poppet are to you."

And she truly did. For, the truth of it was, Joy

was also lonely.

Unbearably so at times.

She missed the other girls' companionship at Haven House and Academy for the Enrichment of Young Women. There'd been no opportunity to make new friends since she'd taken her current position.

Except for Mercy Feathers, she hadn't seen any of her former friends either. Joy did correspond with several. Only sporadically, however, since foolscap, ink, and postage were luxuries she could ill afford, and Mrs. Thackpenny only grudgingly shared the former.

Joy's isolation was especially trying this time of year when evidence of the upcoming Yuletide was everywhere. Why, just yesterday, a gleaming claret-colored coach had trundled by with a festive evergreen, holly, and gold beribboned wreath secured to the back.

Now that person possessed the holiday spirit.

Mrs. Thackpenny didn't observe Christmas-tide with so much as a sprig of mistletoe or a cinnamon bun. Holly and gingerbread were taboo to the crusty widow. On the other hand, Mrs. Shepherd had literally decked the halls, doorways, and mantels of Haven House and Academy for the Enrichment of Young Women.

Such delicious, mouth-watering smells had filled the corridors for days in advance of the holiday. Beaming, she'd present each girl a gift Christmas morning. A festive time was had by all, playing parlor games, singing around the pianoforte, skating on the lake—if the weather cooperated—and of course, eating scrumptious holiday foods.

Joy particularly favored mulled cider and Christmas pudding.

More than once, Joy wondered what her life would have been like if she'd waited for another position to become available. If she hadn't naively believed the false promises Mrs. Thackpenny had made to a young, impressionable girl.

Staring blankly at the heavily draped windows, she lifted a shoulder.

Would I be better off than this life of drudgery?

2

Joy's elderly companion turned her faded blue-eyed gaze upon the blond dachshund snuggled upon a bright pink velvet blanket beside her. Lady Persephone Poppington—Poppet for short—opened sleepy dark brown eyes to stare adoringly at her agitated owner before licking her chops and settling into her comfortable bed once more.

The woman's pets were remarkably loyal. But then, Mrs. Thackpenny had never directed her skin-peeling voice or acrid gaze toward either of them. Instead, she cooed and talked to them as if they were beloved children.

Which, truth be told, Joy supposed to a widow with no offspring of her own, they were.

"Well?" Mrs. Thackpenny snapped, narrowing her eyes to slits and pinning Joy with a reproachful stare. "My Whiskers?"

Though she commanded her focus to remain on Mrs. Thackpenny's disapproving gaze, Joy's attention had a mutinous mind of its own and gravitated lower.

There are at least a half dozen gray, wiry whiskers upon your chin.

Her gaze flew upward, and she bit the inside of her cheek to quell the traitorous smile that dared to try to form.

I am going to burn in hell for my unkindness.

All those years of rigorous lessons on comportment and decorum, not to mention instruction on Christ-like behavior, seemed to have flown from her mind as easily as a wild bird out an open window.

"He was here when I dozed off," Mrs. Thackpenny droned on, patting the stack of cozy throws padding her lap.

Dozed off?

The woman's snoring could've stripped the faded wallpaper from the walls.

Outwardly composed—Joy had, at least, learned *that* skill well at Haven House and Academy for the Enrichment of Young Women—she set aside her embroidery.

"He needed to go outdoors, Mrs. Thackpenny. And after the last incident, I thought it unwise to make him wait."

Three days ago, Whiskers had relieved himself in one of the many cold fireplaces in the townhouse, then proceeded to track ash-covered kitty footprints onto the carpet and sofa. Naturally, Joy had been blamed. Her ill-tempered employer had threatened to reduce her allowance for the cost of cleaning the already stained and shabby cushion and carpet.

Flannery, the sometimes butler, sometimes footman, sometimes coachman and groom, usually saw to the pampered pets' trips outdoors. Only that day, he'd been running an errand for his mistress, and the task had fallen to Joy. Except, her domineering employer hadn't given her a moment's peace since Mrs. Thackpenny had awoken with a headache that morning, and the neglected cat had been entirely forgotten.

Sir Whiskerton had only done what came naturally

An enormous, long-haired white and orange tabby with stunning blue eyes, Sir Galahad Whiskerton—*such a ridiculous name*—behaved more like a dog than a cat. And he quite despised the blue bow his mistress insisted Joy tie about his neck every morning after his breakfast.

The baleful glare the twelve-year-old feline turned upon her made her feel quite guilty. So whenever kippers were served for breakfast, she'd sneak Whiskers hers, as she couldn't abide the nasty things.

Whiskers, on the other hand, had no such aversion. Except for the tails, that was. The cat refused to eat the tails, which meant Joy had to dash about and gather the evidence, less anyone see the proof of her perfidy.

A wry smile bent her mouth as she closed her sewing basket's lid.

She couldn't have fresh tea leaves, but Whiskers sported a new sky-blue silk bow each week and Poppet a peony pink one. Mrs. Thackpenny doted upon her pets, but not her overworked and underpaid staff.

"Go find him," Mrs. Thackpenny ordered.

"I shall fetch him for you at once," Joy said, grateful for the opportunity to stretch her legs.

She just might dally a few minutes and take in Rochester's brisk air. Heavens, how she missed the daily walks relished when still a student at Haven House and Academy for the Enrichment of Young Women.

How had five years gone by so quickly?

So discontentedly?

The laborious passing of each additional year dashing more of her dreams until she feared she'd become a replica of her employer. Disenchanted with life, angry about unfulfilled dreams and deferred hopes, and bitter at God because she was powerless to change a dashed thing.

How long ago that seemed, and how excited she'd been to learn she'd been offered a position as a lady's companion to a granddaughter of an earl. That initial exuberance had wilted, shriveled, and eventually, died.

And yet, what else was Joy to do?

In truth, that plaguing thought had niggled quite persistently of late.

At eight and seventy, Mrs. Thackpenny's

constitution was becoming fragile. When she passed on, Joy would need to find a new position. Mrs. Shepherd would likely help her, but a letter of reference from Mrs. Thackpenny would do much for securing another post.

Only, how did one go about requesting such a thing?

It seemed in grossly poor taste.

By the by, Mrs. Thackpenny. You very well may die soon, and I would like to request a letter of reference so that I might find another position when you shuffle off your mortal coil.

The feisty widow, likely as not, would clock Joy soundly with her scarred cane.

"Ask Mrs. Wilkie for a pot of tea and tray of dainties on your way through the kitchen, Miss Winterborne. Make certain there are peach tarts," Mrs. Thackpenny decreed imperiously, waving said cane in a small arc the way a monarch might brandish a royal mace.

She would've made an impressive queen, wielding her scepter over her subjugated people.

"Then hurry back to help me freshen up," she demanded. "Bring my rosewater and rice powder when you return."

Rosewater and rice powder?

What?

Joy paused at the doorway, casting a puzzled glance at her mistress. "Are you expecting a guest?"

Mrs. Thackpenny rarely entertained. Except for the trio of equally contentious cronies who arrived every second Tuesday for a vicious gossip session. God help any *ton* member they choose to target and shred with their sharp tongues. Joy tried to make herself invisible in a dingy corner, though her ears burned at their blistering rumors and nasty conjectures.

Already stretched to her limit with her cooking and housekeeping responsibilities, Mrs.

Wilkie would be hard-pressed to procure biscuits and sandwiches—*don't forget the peach tarts*—on such short notice.

Since when had Mrs. Thackpenny developed a penchant for peach tarts, of all things?

Her employer cocked her head, and with her wire-rimmed spectacles low on her narrow nose, reminded Joy very much of a quizzical bird.

Except birds didn't look nearly so self-satisfied.

Or wily.

Uneasiness tiptoed across Joy's back from one shoulder to the other.

Precisely *what* was the scheming woman up to?

Mrs. Thackpenny fluttered a knotted, blue-veined hand to the grayish-silver curls framing her face that her black lace cap didn't quite conceal.

"Oh, dear me." She waved her hand and, giving a coquettish smile, fluttered her eyelashes.

"Did I forget to mention Doctor Morrisette is attending me at half-past two?"

Good Lord. Doctor Morrisette?

The very man Joy held in foolish, secret esteem?

Ah, *he* must have a particular fondness for peach tarts.

"I mentioned his visit to Mrs. Wilkie this morning, so she is aware." Mrs. Thackpenny patted her frail chest with a knobby hand. "My cough has worsened, and I fear I may very well be on the brink of lung fever."

Lung fever? Joy nearly rolled her eyes. *If she is on the brink of lung fever, then I am Viscountess Castlereagh.*

Cough. Cough. Cough.

Mrs. Thackpenny proceeded to produce a trio of dry, obviously contrived hacks to emphasize her point. "The good doctor simply *insisted* upon another visit."

And camels dance the minuet.

Joy's gaze flew to the cobalt blue-based ormolu mantle clock.

Five minutes to two.

So much for stealing a few minutes outside.

"I shall return directly."

Keeping her face impassive, Joy gave a small nod before sweeping from the chilly salon. Once in the corridor, she hoisted her skirts and took the stairs two at a time. At best, she'd have ten minutes to improve her appearance before she must return to help Mrs. Thackpenny preen for her esteemed guest.

Flannery could deliver the spoiled puss to his manipulating mistress.

Doctor Morrisette—Lord Brandon *Gorgeous* Morrisette—the third son of a marquess, possessed a devastating smile, which caused her stomach to flip-flop like a panicked trout upon a lake embankment. His arresting deep brown eyes and the shock of dark blond hair that fell rakishly over his brow further enhanced his good looks.

No doctor should be so devastatingly handsome. It couldn't possibly be good for his patients' hearts. Why, Joy would wager her small savings, half his clients—*the female half*—suffered heart palpitations or paroxysms from his presence.

Increasing her pace, Joy mumbled beneath her breath. "He shan't find me wearing my drab gray skirts and covered in orange and white cat hair today."

Which, in point of fact, was how Dr. Morrisette typically found her.

Heat suffused her face that she should even care what he thought of her.

With a single exception, Joy's gowns were ash gray or wren brown. Neither shade suited her coloring but were "perfectly appropriate for a young woman of inferior social standing."

More opinionated words of wisdom from

Mrs. Thackpenny.

Nor would the charming rogue hide a smile, his eyes glinting with amusement as Joy tried to subdue the beastly, yowling cat while the doctor examined his elderly patient.

His patient, who always managed to appear near death's door whenever he was present, but revived as miraculously as Jesus raising Lazarus from the dead the moment the devilishly handsome doctor departed.

And as much as Joy admitted to imprudently admiring the man and his physician's skills, even *he* couldn't be credited with such an astonishing recovery.

As Joy sprinted to her third story chamber, she mentally calculated.

This was the seventh—*no, eighth*—occasion this month the kindly doctor had been imposed upon. The previous months he'd been as frequently inconvenienced by one or another of

Mrs. Thackpenny's contrived ailments. Never had a woman had one foot in the proverbial grave more times than Mrs. Sabella Thackpenny. Much like a cat with multiple lives, she always recovered.

Not that Joy minded Dr. Brandon Morrisette's recurrent calls.

No indeed.

Quite the opposite was true, in fact. The doctor brought news of the outside world and was a refreshing and welcome disruption in her otherwise monotonous routine.

And, yes, Joy secretly admitted, she found him deucedly attractive.

As humiliating as it was to have to greet Doctor Morrisette each time, knowing full well her mistress wasn't nearly as ill as she affected, Joy's heart always leaped. Her pulse quickened in a manner most unsuitable for a proper lady's companion as well.

But Doctor Brandon Morrisette was

masculine perfection, and even an on-the-shelf spinster with no prospects such as herself could appreciate an Adonis in the flesh.

One who always smelled of sandalwood and spices.

Who was she to look a gift horse in the mouth?

That reminded Joy.

She still needed to search Mrs. Thackpenny's bedchamber for whatever medical journal her mistress had acquired and hidden away. She used the book to research diseases and erroneously concluded she suffered from a myriad of them. Combined with the woman's ever-declining eyesight and inability to read well, the diagnoses were becoming increasingly ludicrous.

As she dashed along, Joy rolled her eyes ceilingward and, shaking her head in remembered chagrin, groaned aloud.

Dear Lord above.

Last week, the woman was in a complete dither, absolutely positive that she suffered from Peyronie's disease. Did she simply find a unique or frightening sounding affliction in the medical book, and her failing eyesight prevented her from reading the actual symptoms?

Quite possibly, truth be told.

Mrs. Thackpenny's vision had grown so impaired this past year that Joy read to her on most occasions, and that included bills from her few creditors and even fewer correspondents.

She could only applaud Doctor Morrisette's professionalism as he'd gently explained to the overwrought woman that he was one hundred percent certain, Mrs. Thackpenny did not have the affliction. Furthermore, he'd assured her that only men could acquire that particular disease.

He hadn't elucidated how he could be so confident in his assessment, and given the distinct jollity glimmering in his lovely, chocolate-brown eyes, Joy hadn't dared to ask.

"Are you quite certain, Doctor?" Mrs. Thackpenny quavered, her eyes owlishly large behind her spectacles.

"Absolutely," came the doctor's solemn reply.

Jaw clenched against the cold, Joy skidded into her sparsely furnished chamber and yanked her favorite gown from the wardrobe. A deep blue wool trimmed at the bodice and sleeves in crocheted lace, the fabric made her eyes bluer, her skin appear creamier, and brought out the pale honey tones in her bright coppery hair.

Shivering, her teeth chattering, Joy grumbled softly as she pulled the ugly gray gown over her head and threw it unceremoniously upon the bare floor. Someday, somehow, she was going to live someplace warm and not wear drab, earth-colored gowns.

In fact, she'd only wear jeweled tones.

She had no control over any of that right

now. But by thunder, today the handsome doctor would not laugh at her again.

3

His physician's bag in one hand, Doctor Brandon Morrisette briskly rapped the knocker upon the faded, paint-chipped green door with the other. When he'd received Mrs. Sabella Thackpenny's missive this morning, requesting he listen to her lungs again, he'd nearly sent a note around refusing her entreaty.

By God, during his last visit, she'd coyly asked him to examine her cossetted dog and cat.

Egads, her cat and dog!

Just as he'd been about to politely decline and explain there were animal doctors for such things, he'd caught Miss Joy Winterborne's wide-eyed glance.

Something in those expressive hydrangea-blue eyes, rimmed with sooty, gold-tipped lashes, had given him pause. Had, in truth, made him consider if Joy would be on the receiving end of her mistress's tetchy temper if he didn't oblige the elderly matron's ridiculous request.

And why it should matter to him if Miss Joy Winterborne were distressed, Brandon couldn't conceive. But it did, in truth, and a great deal more than it ought to. Something more than a physician's empathy compelled him to act as a buffer between her and her employer.

He felt confident he'd hit upon the truth when he'd agreed to examine the pets and seen the relief flood Miss Winterborne's pretty features. She swiftly schooled her too-thin, too pale face into a mask of neutrality, but those magnificent eyes of hers fairly glowed with appreciation and gratitude.

Suddenly, he'd found himself very much wanting to make her happy. To see that small, enigmatic upward sweep of her full, peach lips if only for the briefest of moments. No, he yearned to see her genuine smile—a full-mouthed, humor-filled grin.

Directed toward him.

You've taken leave of your bloody senses, Brandon Fullerton Wesley Morrisette.

He blamed his befuddlement on too many long nights tending the sick paupers and beggars at St. Peter's Home for the Impoverished and Infirm. An establishment very much in need of additional benefactors and the financial support of philanthropical souls if it were to remain open.

It must remain open.

Too many unfortunate souls had nowhere else to turn for help.

Mayhap, Mrs. Thackpenny could be persuaded to part with a few coins, especially during this celebratory time of year when need and want seemed all that much more prevalent. He would apply to her Christian charity. Surely she couldn't refuse him then.

Keeping that notion at the forefront of his mind, Brandon had listened to the dog's and cat's hearts, peered in their hostile eyes, peeked in their ears and mouths—receiving a nip from Poppet and a scratch from Whiskers for his efforts—and declared them fit as fiddles.

In truth, the pets were aging too, and a modified diet and increased exercise wouldn't go amiss for either. A healthier menu, more fresh fruits and vegetables, and increased activity for Mrs. Thackpenny and Miss Winterborne as well, he'd advised.

Mrs. Thackpenny had responded to his recommendations with a bland stare.

The sly old bird didn't fool him for an instant.

Yes, she was elderly, and her eyesight was significantly diminished. And yes, she suffered from arthritis, and her lungs weren't as healthy as they once had been. And yes, the same could be said of her heart. Nonetheless, the elderly dame wasn't ready to cock up her toes or put her spoon in the wall just yet.

Today, Brandon intended to insist upon dietary and exercise changes for the entire household as part of his treatment regimen. He also hoped to prevail upon Mrs. Thackpenny's benevolence on behalf of St. Peter's Home for the Impoverished and Infirm.

Using his charm and a roguish smile to persuade her wasn't beyond him either.

To gain her cooperation, Brandon was also prepared to declare he'd be required to attend Mrs. Thackpenny twice weekly to observe her progress.

And Joy's as well.

Truth be told, it was partially because of her grateful glances at his last visit that he'd agreed to come today.

Simply put, Brandon wanted to see her again.

If it meant indulging her manipulative mistress, he didn't mind as long as Mrs. Thackpenny's demands didn't interfere with the treatment and care of his other patients.

In the seven months since he'd taken over Doctor Daggat's practice and inherited Mrs. Thackpenny as a patient, Brandon had often wondered what circumstances had compelled Miss Winterborne to become a companion to the tight-fisted curmudgeon.

Mrs. Thackpenny's worth wasn't precisely a topic of conversation in the *beau monde's* most elite drawing rooms or ballrooms, but her sizeable fortune *was* the envy of many peers.

For all of Joy's patience and attentiveness to her aged employer, her straight back, squared shoulders, and what *might* be considered an obstinate tilt to her delicate chin, indicated that Miss Joy Winterborne possessed a fiery spirit beneath her outwardly serene façade.

The sparks glinting in her brilliant blue eyes gave her away as well. Still, one had to observe her carefully to detect the almost imperceptible gleam of mutiny within their captivating depths. She guarded her secret well, as if afraid of discovery by her employer.

He had a hunch Mrs. Thackpenny wouldn't appreciate a spitfire or a hellion for a companion. Although—he grinned—that interaction might be quite entertaining to observe.

Even Doctor Daggat had warned Brandon of the contentious Mrs. Thackpenny and also advised him to request payment at the time services were rendered. Or he'd likely never receive them.

It baffled him how she could be so stingy

when she had plenty, while others survived on so very little. Charity obviously didn't begin at home under Mrs. Thackpenny's roof.

That was one of the reasons he'd chosen to pursue medicine rather than a career in the military or church, as was generally expected from nobles' younger sons. Besides not having the temperament for either, he believed he could do more good for mankind as a physician.

It wasn't that Brandon didn't have a strong belief in God or that he didn't attend Sunday services regularly. Being a man of the cloth wasn't his calling, and he'd known it from a young age. The military held even less appeal for a man who wanted to heal people.

Father hadn't been pleased. Not at all. Nevertheless, in the end, he'd given Brandon his blessing. He'd paid for Brandon's education, and until his death two years ago, Father had even contributed funds to St. Peter's House for the

Impoverished and Infirm every quarter.

Brandon seriously doubted Mrs. Thackpenny would be as generous. Few of those blessed with great wealth were generous with their riches. According to Doctor Daggat, Mrs. Thackpenny was amongst those who hated to part with her coin.

When billed for his services, she was known to have sent Doctor Daggat leftover kidney or shepherd's pie, a half-drunk bottle of wine, stale bread, a hideous needlepoint footstool, calf's foot jelly procured from God only knew where, and once, a moth-eaten cloak. Daggat vowed the garment had been her husband's, dead these past five decades.

Why the devil isn't anyone answering the door?

Shifting his feet against the blistering cold, Brandon lifted his hand to knock again when the door finally swung open, creaking and scraping on unoiled hinges.

"Doctor Morrisette."

A rather breathless, fresh-faced Miss Joy Winterborne greeted him with a winsome smile that stole the air from his lungs for a heartbeat.

"Forgive me for making you wait. I was, um…" She pressed a long-fingered hand to her trim middle, her throat working as she swallowed. "That is to say, we were making preparations for your visit."

She glanced down self-consciously and brushed at the vibrant blue of her gown. Color bloomed across the delicate slope of her high cheekbones.

By Jove, she is blushing.

Because she'd anticipated his calling today?

Well, now, wasn't that an unexpected but most excellent turn of events?

Primal male satisfaction winged through Brandon's veins, heating his blood as a grin tugged the edges of his mouth upward.

This was the first time he'd seen Joy in anything other than dreary gray or dull brown frocks, and he couldn't help but admire the becoming color on her. The hue did remarkable things to her glorious hair—the shade somewhere between a shimmering, coppery gold and rich, warm honey.

The long-sleeved gown hugged the gentle swells of her bosom and emphasized her tiny waist before flowing to the floor in a swirl of midnight. She'd secured a silver brooch atop the lace at her throat.

All in all, Miss Joy Winterborne looked very fetching, indeed.

"You are looking very well today." He flashed her the practiced smile he used to calm nervous patients. "Is that a new gown?"

Her impossibly blue eyes went round, and her tongue darted out to wet the seam of her plump lips.

That was unforeseen and wholly telling as well.

The minx was as aware of Brandon as a man as he was of her as a very appealing woman.

"No." She shook her head and snagged her lower lip between her neat white teeth as if to prevent herself from saying more.

Heaven help him, for the desire to taste that sweet mouth slammed into him with such unexpected force, Brandon felt as awkward as a first-year medical student. That his blood heated further condemned him as an inexperienced beginner.

No, blister it, he felt as inept and clumsy as when he'd lost his virginity at sixteen to the buxom, older parlor maid who'd been flirting with him for months. What Brandon had lacked in finesse he'd made up for in endurance, and he and Marissa had enjoyed each other that summer until he'd gone off to university.

She'd been Brandon's one and only lover, for he'd found he didn't have the disposition for casual intimate encounters. They seemed shallow, and though his view was unpopular, he'd always believed sex was an expression of love. Not just a carnal urge.

Later, as a physician, his knowledge of the havoc sexually transmitted diseases wreaked upon humans kept him from jumping in and out of beds with the same proclivity as many of his friends.

For that matter, his older brothers, too, before they'd wed.

He couldn't count the times he'd been mocked for his abstinence and had long since developed a tough hide regarding the ribbing.

Setting his well-used brown leather bag on the half-table, the only piece of furniture in the entry other than a slightly lopsided straight back chair, Brandon examined the dim interior.

He'd never seen it otherwise.

Always dull and gloomy and fusty.

So unlike the vibrant woman beside him with her reddish-blond hair and sparkling blue eyes fringed by thick lashes. She should be surrounded by color and light.

"I hope you didn't become chilled while waiting," she murmured before giving him an unconstrained, breathtaking smile.

That simple upward bend of her mouth directed toward him scattered his wits. The wintery breeze blew them like thistledown, pell-mell along the lane. His attention remained riveted on her tempting, parted lips as his mind pondered if they'd taste of peaches and cream.

"Doctor?"

Her winged reddish eyebrows puzzled together, she gazed at him expectantly, one arm extended and indicating he should enter the house.

Brandon scrambled to come back to himself and recall what she'd said.

Chilled.

Yes, she fretted that he'd taken a chill.

In truth, he was more likely to do so inside the house, which, in his experience, was always underheated.

"It's of no matter." Forcing a nonchalant smile, he stepped across the threshold. "It's a fine day outside."

If you could count a cold, blustery December day as such. Nonetheless, the sun valiantly shone through the few scattered pewter clouds, and the wind but teased rather than blew with any real determination to cause discomfort.

Joy peered past him, a wistful expression skittering across her face. "It does look to be so."

She glanced upward, meeting his eyes, and he noticed the dark blue ring around her iris. It was exactly the same shade as her gown. She had quite the loveliest eyes, and he found himself boldly staring. A man could drown in those sapphire depths and not mind it in the least.

"Even though I don't like the cold, I've always liked the winter, especially when it snows." She raised one sloping shoulder and inch. "I suppose it's because I was born in December."

Winterborne.

"Your birthday is this month?"

"Yes, the seventeenth."

Assessing her, he narrowed his eyes the merest bit.

How old was Miss Joy Winterborne anyway?

Running his gaze over her face, Brandon examined the creamy skin, the clear blue eyes, and the aristocratic bone structure.

Somewhere in the middle of her third decade, he decided.

Had her family fallen on hard financial times, and she'd been obligated to find employment? If so, hers was a common enough tale.

"Mine is in January," he offered conversationally. "The twentieth. I shall be one and thirty."

Brandon passed her his hat and gloves, and finally, his outercoat before retrieving his doctor's bag. He disliked treating her as a servant, but the manservant who sometimes acted as Mrs. Thackpenny's butler was nowhere to be seen this day.

"I'll be five and twenty," Joy murmured, the merest hint of despair leeching into her modulated tone.

Still staring out the door, she stood there, his garments in her arms. There was such yearning in her spectacular eyes that he impetuously blurted, "Miss Winterborne, perhaps you'd care to take a walk when I'm done examining Mrs. Thackpenny?"

4

Joy swung her astonished gaze to Brandon and then veered her attention to the open door once more.

"I would, in truth." She carefully set his possessions on the table before facing him. "However, I fear Mrs. Thackpenny wouldn't permit it. Particularly not if it isn't Saturday and my half-day off."

Her disappointment was tangible, and it stirred protective instincts quite different than those Brandon typically felt toward his patients.

"Hmm, even if I prescribed it for your

health?" He fell into step beside her.

She sent him a sideways glance, and a small smile touched her lips. "Is that even a legitimate prescription?"

"It is if I say so," he responded easily.

Her movements were unhurried and fluid. That of a woman of natural grace or one who'd been trained to move with feminine precision. Her speech and manners indicated she'd received an education, but she remained an enigma.

Brandon quite enjoyed riddles, and he meant to solve the puzzle that was Joy Winterborne.

"Surely, she wants her companion hale and hardy," he persisted, astonished at his own doggedness even as he spoke.

"Doctor Morrisette, in point of fact, she cares more for her pampered dog and cat than she does for me." Eyes wide and horrified, Joy slapped a delicate hand over her mouth as if suddenly appreciating how disloyal and critical she sounded.

"I beg your pardon, Doctor. That was most inappropriate. Forgive my outburst, please."

A hint of trepidation touched the outer edges of her eyes as if she worried he'd reveal her forwardness to her employer, and she'd summarily be dismissed for speaking out of turn.

"I quite agree. They are the most spoiled of pets." Winking, he kicked his mouth up into a sideways grin. "Please tell me I am not expected to examine them again today. They are not the most congenial of patients."

She chuckled, a husky, melodic sound that at once made him wonder what she'd sound like in his bed as he made love to her.

Fiend seize it.

Control yourself, man.

Such lustful thoughts were not typical for him, and a wave of shame heated his neck.

"No, Doctor. I don't believe Mrs.

Thackpenny intends for you to exam her pets today."

They'd almost reached the stairs, and he turned to ascend them as he had dozens of times prior. Joy, however, remained at the foot of the stairway.

"Mrs. Thackpenny will see you in the parlor today."

A distinct twinkle glittered in Joy's eyes, and her mouth twitched the merest bit. Hands clasped demurely before her like a virtuous novice, she spoke in a servant's neutral tones.

Tones which did nothing to disguise the hilarity shining in her eyes.

She's laughing at me, the minx.

"She's requested tea and dainties for your, ah, *visit.*" An almost imperceptible warble in Joy's voice revealed the mirth she subdued.

Blister and blast.

Mrs. Thackpenny had migrated from not-so-subtle scheming to outright machinations.

Eyes narrowed in contemplation, he tapped his fingertips atop his bag.

To what purpose?

Well, two could play at that game.

Arching an eyebrow, Brandon shifted his bag to his other hand and cast a glance farther down the corridor.

"I take it she's not unwell then? Or at least not as indisposed as she'd led me to believe?"

It was Joy's turn to quirk a coppery-bronze eyebrow. "Well, as you are well aware, Doctor, she has numerous maladies on any given day. Of late, it's a slight cough and…"

She pinkened, and a blush stained her milky cheeks again—*peaches and cream*—as her gaze skittered away from his.

Peaches were his favorite fruit. And with her reddish-blond hair, satiny skin, and that delectable seam of her two plump lips, she reminded him very much of a ripe peach. One he craved to taste.

He swiftly turned his mind to less appealing notions, less his wayward musings lead down a very unprofessional pathway.

Mrs. Thackpenny.

Yes. That would do the trick.

Turning his attention to his patient effectively doused his ill-timed ardor. Joy had said she suffered from another ailment besides coughing.

"And?" he coaxed, once more matching Joy's pace as she led him to the heretofore never seen parlor. He'd only ever been permitted into the entry, the upstairs corridor, and Mrs. Thackpenny's bedchamber filled with ancient furniture, liberally covered in cat hair.

As they walked, he continued to peruse his surroundings.

Even though Christmas was but a fortnight away, nothing indicated the holiday was observed in this household. He'd spend Christmastide with his oldest brother Conner, the current Marquess of Rockford, along with Conner's wife and their three offspring. Their middle brother, Randal, and his wife, and son would also be there.

All in all, the holiday was always a pleasant experience and even included a Christmas Eve ball.

Brandon was grateful Conner held the festivities at Rockford Park, a few miles outside of Rochester, rather than at one of his other estates or in London. It saved Brandon from having to choose between spending the holiday with his family, whom he loved and whose company he enjoyed, and his patients who might need him.

Brandon eyed Joy, who still hadn't responded to his earlier prompting.

She was silent for so long, he thought she was too overcome by embarrassment to answer him. Was Mrs. Thackpenny still going on about Peyronie's Disease? How she'd even been aware of the affliction, he couldn't begin to venture.

At last, Joy spoke, keeping her focus straight ahead, allowing him to admire her profile. Choosing her words with care, she said, "She is having increasingly loud and ever more distressing…*digestive*…issues."

He stared at her for a long moment—*she truly has the most adorable nose*—and then understanding dawned as her words finally sunk in. Brandon nearly laughed aloud but managed to check his hilarity by putting a closed fist to his mouth and clearing his throat. "Ahem."

Such delicate things were *never* discussed with the opposite sex.

"Ah. I see. A dietary change may be in order."

"Indeed." Laughter tinged Joy's voice once more.

He'd love to hear her unfettered laughter. She'd only ever smiled at him.

"She should find relief in a day or two if she

follows my advice."

What was it about this woman that distracted him so?

Had him engaging in wicked imaginations?

"I'd be ever so grateful. As would Poppet and Whiskers. Her, ah, *outbursts*, quite terrify them."

His shoulders shaking, a deep-throated chuckle escaped Brandon.

By Zeus, she was delightful and utterly unpretentious.

Even though he was the third son, more women than he could count had attempted to catch his eye and win his favor, simply to associate themselves with the Morrisette name. More aptly, the Rockford marquessate. It didn't seem to matter that he was presently fifth in queue for the title. If his brothers sired more sons, he'd move farther down that line. That truth didn't matter to him one whit.

At the salon's entrance, Brandon touched

Joy's arm. "I am sincere about my offer to take the air with you. I would truly consider it a privilege. I'll wait until your half-day if I must."

Had four days ever seemed so far away?

"You may ask her, but I fully expect she'll refuse." Joy searched his face, her eyes a warm, visual caress. Resignation cast a slight shadow over her features.

She fully expected Mrs. Thackpenny to object to her taking the air with him.

Joy isn't a bloody prisoner here.

He clamped his teeth, straining to prevent the harsh words from exploding from his mouth. In truth, Joy *was* little more than a prisoner of her circumstances.

Though it was none of his business, Brandon meant to change that.

A faint constellation of cinnamon-colored freckles dusted Joy's nose and cheeks, and feminine interest sparked in the depths of her eyes as she observed him. If Brandon weren't mistaken—and he was quite certain he wasn't—something more lingered in the captivating blue pools as well.

Something she was afraid to express.

One way or another, he'd wriggle permission from her impossible employer to take Miss Joy Winterborne for a stroll.

Grinning, Brandon took Joy's elbow, noting once more that she was too thin. He also meant to remedy that, intrusive or not. He lowered his head conspiratorially. The aroma of soap, lemon, and Joy's essence met his nostrils.

Clean and warm and womanly. As fresh, appealing, and unpretentious as the lady herself.

"Not if I prescribe a daily constitutional for her health and insist I accompany her to ensure she obeys my directives." He slanted her a sideways, sheepish glance. "I believe she may have developed a *tendre* for me, and I mean to exploit it for hers and your benefit. I could also agree to come for tea again if that would persuade her to cooperate."

He'd agree to nearly anything to see Joy.

From the first time he'd laid eyes on her, he'd admired her self-possession and kindness. But she'd also sparked a fire in him few women—*no women*—had for a very long while.

"Is that fair to her?" She caught the inside of her cheek between her teeth. Her uncertainty was as adorable as was her sincere concern for her undeserving mistress. "That is, to intentionally encourage her…ah…feelings, even if they are out of place?"

He touched her satiny cheek with his bent forefinger, and a tiny gasp escaped her petal-pink parted lips.

"My dear Miss Winterborne, it's your feelings that intrigue me."

5

The Vines Gardens

Rochester, England

18 December 1817-Mid-morning

J oy darted a surreptitious glance to the strikingly
tall man strolling at her side. She couldn't seem
to help herself. Brandon Morrisette was a
masculine magnet, and she was but a hapless
female unable to withstand his irresistible draw.

A moth to the flame and all of that cliché
twaddle.

Cutting him what she hoped were unnoticed

sidelong glances from beneath her lashes, she furtively studied him as they walked along.

Brandon's midnight blue caped greatcoat hugged his broad shoulders, the high collar brushing his slightly too long walnut blond hair. The fine wool slapped against his glossy Hessians as he tempered his stride to match that of the elderly woman clutching his arm.

Joy considered his aristocratic features.

They weren't all harsh angles and planes, but the strong slope of his square chin— marred by a small white scar—gave way to chiseled cheeks and a high brow.

Was the scar the result of a boyhood injury?

He'd have been a beautiful child, and the yearning for a babe of her own nearly cleaved her heart in two. Companions—*spinsters*—didn't have children.

Purposefully refocusing her attention on him to divert herself from her melancholy, she roved her gaze over his face again. Fine lines etched the corners of his lovely deep brown eyes as if he smiled often.

Joy knew that to be true from the times he'd doctored Mrs. Thackpenny.

Her silly heart palpitated in remembrance of that curved mouth after he'd announced it was *her* feelings that intrigued him. And devil take Doctor Brandon Morrisette, she'd wondered for a week what, exactly, he'd meant by that tantalizing remark.

A tiny, appreciative smile bent her mouth.

Lean, sinewy masculinity.

That was what Brandon was, and she was only mortal, after all.

Joy hadn't even attempted to resist his charm.

Why deny herself this momentary happiness?

She'd had little enough of it these past five years.

Brandon's brushed felt top hat, slanted at a

rakish angle, gave him a dashing air as he nodded now and again to curious acquaintances of his that they encountered along the wintery broad walk.

He offered neither an introduction nor an explanation, for which Joy was exceedingly grateful. Though she was appreciative of her position, no matter how politely worded, the role of companion held stigma.

Poor or unwanted relation.

Spinster.

Unmarriageable.

Dependent upon others.

A person to pity while being heartily grateful you were not she.

Surely if they had not already, the doctor, Mrs. Thackpenny, and Joy would soon become the topic of many a drawing room conversation. Those they encountered on their strolls would try to contrive a logical reason why the handsome third son of a marquess should be attending the crotchety Mrs. Thackpenny and her mouse of a companion. Neither of whom was often seen in public and never in the company of a man. Let alone a rascally charmer such as he.

Joy walked Poppet, who, despite having endured a lead few times previously, behaved remarkably well. But then, the poor dear was ten years old and her little legs so short, she had to trot to keep up with Brandon's sedate pace.

The plane trees' gnarled, barren branches extended over the level footpath, a testament to the season. And yet, despite the cold, Joy felt a giddy warmth, through and through.

She well knew the reason.

The virile man so close, she could reach out and touch him should she wish.

And Joy did wish. She wished very much, indeed.

For a week now, Brandon had called as promised. Promptly at eleven every morning.

These past two days, Mrs. Thackpenny had been waiting impatiently in the corridor for his arrival.

Such a transformation had come over the woman, Joy was uncertain what to make of the astounding change. Even now, as Mrs. Thackpenny hobbled along, the sour-tempered dame she'd known for five years appeared—*happy*. Truly happy.

A droll papery cackle slipping past her lips at something Brandon murmured, Mrs. Thackpenny grasped his elbow and employed her cane with the skill of a cavalry officer.

Joy had been utterly flabbergasted when with reasonably little effort, he'd coaxed the contrary woman into agreeing to take the air with him for half an hour each day. One half an hour, which had stretched into at least an hour daily and included an outing with Joy on her half-day to Barclay's Book Shoppe and Emporium.

Brandon looked too pleased with himself by

far, and if Joy hadn't been so eager to accompany them, she might've thought him arrogant.

Each day, he arrived in his carriage. And each day, he toted an armful of packages inside, which he encouraged Mrs. Thackpenny to open.

Prescriptions, he called them.

What a load of blatant fustian rubbish, but Joy adored him all the more for it.

After an expected pretense at fussing and objecting, Mrs. Thackpenny had eagerly unwrapped the first parcel, only needing Joy's assistance to help untangle a knot in the string.

Delicious foods and what Brandon deemed *essential* holiday decorations filled the brown paper wrapped boxes. A ham, ginger biscuits, Shrewsbury biscuits, maid of honor tarts, pies, sweetbreads, puddings, and much, much more.

Flannery and Mrs. Wilkie had nearly wept in appreciation.

For once, the entire household was in danger

of becoming plump.

That first day, Brandon had brought swags of pine boughs and holly for the fireplace mantels in the salon and dining room.

"What are you trying to do, you impudent bacon-brain?" Mrs. Thackpenny had snapped. "I don't observe the holiday," she'd harrumphed, glaring at him with her arms folded.

He'd blithely ignored her and called upon Flannery and Mrs. Wilkie to help him and Joy display the garlands. Mrs. Thackpenny, despite her grumblings, had pointed her cane several times, directing the foursome to raise one side or lower another.

The second day, Mrs. Thackpenny, after turning a starchy eye upon a grinning Brandon and muttering, "Insolent rapscallion," had whisked open a box of vibrant cranberry-red and gold bows.

Naturally, Brandon set Joy and the delighted

servants to tying them upon the sconces, lamp bases, and banister. Lady Persephone Poppington and Sir Galahad Whiskerton also found themselves festooned with a merry Christmas bow each.

A degree of festiveness had crept into nearly every corner of the previously depressing house, and it was all due to Brandon Morrisette. If Joy believed in such nonsense, she'd suspect he possessed magical powers, for what he'd achieved with Mrs. Thackpenny was nothing short of miraculous.

How he had wheedled his way into the contrary woman's good graces, she couldn't quite say. But the menu had improved, and Mrs. Thackpenny now actually permitted fires in all of the occupied rooms. In truth, the past week had been the most enjoyable of Joy's life since leaving Haven House and Academy for the Enrichment of Young Women. It wasn't just the improvement in her living conditions either.

Today, the darling man had dragged a kissing bough and sprigs of mistletoe out of the boxes he'd brought.

Mrs. Thackpenny astonished Joy by clapping her hands and laughing out loud.

Mrs. Thackpenny did not laugh.

Neither did she clap her hands with the exuberance of an excited child.

Indeed. Brandon Morrisette was either a miracle worker or a wizard.

Mrs. Thackpenny had then proceeded to regale them with a tale of how she'd met her dearly departed husband at a Christmastide house party. When he'd stolen a kiss beneath a kissing bough, she'd lost her heart to him.

Joy's heart twinged at the obvious love the old woman had felt for her husband. She'd loved him so deeply and wholly, she'd never remarried. In time her bereavement and loss had turned her bitter and caustic.

But since Brandon had begun paying marked attention to her, charming her with his gentle humor and considerate bedside manner, the hard shell she'd protected herself with for five decades had begun crumbling away.

Sniffling, Mrs. Thackpenny fished around inside her sleeve in search of one of the many handkerchiefs Joy had embroidered for her. A wistful smile framing her mouth, she'd daintily dabbed beneath her spectacles.

Joy's gaze had meshed with Brandon's, and an electrical current had charged between them despite the several feet that separated them.

He'd given the kissing bough a pointed look and then winked at her.

Joy's all too eager imagination had run amuck this past hour, trying to determine precisely what he'd alluded to.

Surely, he hadn't meant he'd like to kiss *her*?

At the thought, her heart tumbled over itself, and she very nearly missed a step.

Every year, for as long as Joy could recall, she'd made a wish on Christmas Eve.

Oh, she'd stopped believing they'd actually come to pass many, many years ago. Regardless, what harm was there in wishing? Sometimes, especially these past five years, she had a hard time deciding what to wish for.

Not this year.

No indeed.

This year, she knew precisely what her Christmas wish—*prayer*—would be.

6

If miracles were truly possible and if God could hear the cry of Joy's heart, if the stars aligned just right, and if the Almighty bestowed even the tiniest amount of grace upon her, Joy would wish Brandon felt the same way about her as she did him.

How often had she wondered what it would be like to be kissed? More specifically, these past six months, what would it be like to have Brandon settle his sculpted mouth upon hers?

Would his lips be soft?

Firm? Velvety?

What would they taste like?

The spices that always wafted from him?

Coffee?

Perhaps brandy or tobacco?

"Shall we return?" Brandon eyed the sky, a crease drawing his slanted eyebrows together. He met her eyes. "I fear we will be rained upon if we do not hurry."

"Hmph. A little rain never hurt anyone," Mrs. Thackpenny declared, beating the pavement with her cane. "In fact, I'd wager it would be quite amusing watching those preening hens ogling you yonder, Doctor Morrisette, wilt from the precipitation."

The four young women were indisputably lovely in their expensive redingotes and elegant bonnets. Two even carried matching fur-lined muffs and wore half-boots in the same colors—coordinated elegance and perfection.

Joy glanced down at her serviceable steel-gray

cloak, noting the carefully stitched repairs and occasional moth hole. Her scuffed half-boots peeked at her from beneath the frayed hem, and she'd knitted her mittens herself from leftover yarn. Her bonnet was the same one she'd had when she left Haven House. A simple navy-blue affair without a single adornment.

Everything she owned was plain and serviceable.

All of which served to make her feel an absolute frump and far beneath the darling debutantes' touch. Brandon's too, although he'd never indicated in word or deed that he regarded her as inferior.

It was the knowledge of her paternity that convicted her.

His father was a marquess.

Yours might be as well.

Ah, but that was the crux of it, wasn't it?

Legitimacy trumped all in his world.

Character. Morality. Kindness. Generosity. Integrity.

Every deuced thing—good or bad.

All because of chance or fate, or whatever divine force one wanted to credit with why one person was born into wealth and privilege. And another, through no fault of their own, was cast into poverty and hardship.

The quartet released a chorus of grating giggles, and Joy regarded them, mindful to keep her expression benign. The strain of keeping her facial muscles in a relaxed, pleasant mien might very well lead to the headache of the century, however.

A piercing twist of something which she very much feared might be jealousy twisted in her abdomen. Even her most elegant gown, the blue woolen, was far inferior to the quality of their garments, and her hair had never been arranged into an intricate coiffeur. A simple chignon was all she could manage on her own.

Orphans and lady's maids don't dress like the first tulip of fashion.

The truth of that observation only served to remind her of her station.

An unwanted bastard daughter.

Someone's shame and disgrace, cast off and hidden away.

Yes, but one of her parents—she'd likely never know which—had cared enough to see her raised in comfort and had provided an education and occupation. They must've cared a little about her.

Mustn't they?

Heads together, a hint of perfectly formed ringlets framing equally porcelain complexions, dainty upturned noses, and cupid's bow mouths, the quartet giggled again, drawing Joy back to the present.

They stared at Brandon with hungry, inviting

gazes.

Gazes perhaps not entirely as innocent as they ought to have been.

He, on the other hand, appeared oblivious to their blatant posing and seductive wiles. Not once did he glance in their direction.

"Shall we head for home, then? While we were gone, I arranged to have mulled cider prepared and roasted chestnuts and a yule log delivered."

Oh, the precious, wonderful man.

He looked at Joy while he spoke, his mesmerizing chocolatey brown gaze holding hers captive.

If Joy hadn't already given him her heart, she would've done so at that moment.

Wholly and irrevocably.

In passing, during one of their walks, she mentioned she hadn't enjoyed mulled cider or roasted chestnuts for many years. Not since leaving Haven House and Academy for the Enrichment of Young Women, truth to tell. It was that day a street vendor had been selling chestnuts near The Vines.

And Brandon had remembered her offhand comment.

"That sounds lovely." She should look away before her employer noticed their locked gazes. Before those uppity twits lusting after Brandon also took note.

But dash her for a fool, she couldn't.

"Miss Winterborne. What say you?" *Thwack* went Mrs. Thackpenny's cane upon the pavement, breaking the romantic spell.

Joy blinked, and drawing a steadying breath, gathered her composure. "I beg your pardon?"

The widow cackled wickedly and shoved her spectacles up her nose. "Will that bothersome foursome, who haven't a brain betwixt them all, gamble with the elements and linger to gawp at *our* dear doctor a jot longer?"

Our doctor?

Joy's attention shot to Brandon's, her gaze crashing into his once more.

His smoldering eyes—good Lord, she might very well incinerate on the spot—bored into hers—a question sparking in his. Carnal awareness swept her, and a sensual jolt raised every pore from her scalp to the soles of her feet.

She recognized what his gaze silently asked, and it astounded her that she did, for Joy was not a worldly woman.

He wanted to know.

Was he *her* doctor?

She very much wanted him to be, and not for treatment of any malady either.

Except, perhaps, to run those large hands over her as he explained the cause of her palpating heart, the heat tunneling through her veins, her knees gone to jelly, and the sweet heaviness low in her belly.

Warmth suffused her cheeks at her wanton thoughts. Thoughts, which she was positive no good Christian woman ought to have and which she was equally positive Brandon knew very well tripped about her mind.

Lady Persephone Poppington abruptly jerked her lead as she attempted to charge after a red squirrel, saving Joy the humiliation of anyone discovering her heart's secret. She swiftly bent and lifted the wriggling, yipping dachshund into her arms.

"Hush. You are ever so much larger than that poor little thing." The squirrel tore up the nearest tree, where it quivered in fright, flicking its tail. "See, you've scared it, Poppet."

Joy sent Brandon a glance, only to find him watching her with such intensity, he might as well have reached out and touched her.

Yes, he knew her wicked, wicked thoughts.

He cleared his throat and directed his regard overhead in what she was sure was feigned concern over the weather.

"I think we are wiser than they, Mrs. Thackpenny," Joy finally said after her employer looked between Joy and Brandon three times. "And we should heed Doctor Morrisette's sage advice. It wouldn't do for you to become wet and catch a chill."

"Poppycock. We are both made of sterner stuff than that, Miss Winterborne."

A week ago, Joy wouldn't have said as much about her employer. But today, she heartily agreed.

The widow pointed her cane in Joy's direction. "However, I should like to sample the mulled wine though it's scarcely past noon. It's been decades since I've indulged." She peered up at Brandon, a twinkle in her faded eyes despite her downward turned mouth. "I believe you are trying to corrupt me, young rascal."

He winked and, leaning down, waggled his eyebrows. "Am I succeeding?"

"We shall see." Mrs. Thackpenny released another raspy chuckle, more color in her deeply lined face than Joy could ever recall seeing. "We shall see."

"In all seriousness, however. I wish to escort you to my carriage," Brandon intoned, steering them toward the waiting conveyance, which always contained several heavy lap robes. "I would blame myself should either of you become ill."

"Hmph." Mrs. Thackpenny blew out a hefty, contemptuous snort. "You are the one who ordered me to take a daily constitutional, my good man. Didn't *you* consider I might take ill?"

"That would be a monumental catastrophe. I still have several holiday surprises to confer upon you." Extending his elbow to Joy, Brandon cocked his eyebrows at Mrs. Thackpenny then gave her a devilish wink. "Before I'm through, Madam, you shall anticipate Christmas as much as I."

"You young scamp." She bounced her cane off his leg but not hard enough to do him any injury. "I'm far too old to fall for your charms. Save them for a younger, more deserving gel. Although I don't mind your flattery or attempts to sway me with your smiles and smooth words."

She speared a considering glance toward Joy, who managed to keep her face impassive.

But only just.

Did her employer suspect Joy's affection for Brandon?

Was Mrs. Thackpenny testing her?

Seeing if Joy's moral character was above reproach?

Honestly, she didn't know what to think of Sabella Thackpenny's behavior anymore.

Such a change had occurred in the woman these past few days, Joy had to wonder at it. Were kindness and attention all that she had needed these many years?

Hadn't Joy bestowed those upon her?

Yes, but perhaps Mrs. Thackpenny believed it was only because Joy was required to do so as her paid companion and doubted her sincerity.

Brandon raised and lowered his elbow, a silent request for Joy to take it.

Joy tentatively laid her fingertips on his forearm, delighting in the way his muscles flexed at her touch.

During their prior walks, she'd trailed him and Mrs. Thackpenny down the paths, mindful of her inferior station. For whatever reason, Brandon had decided to make a public display and change that.

She hoped, against hope, that perhaps that meant he felt something toward her too.

7

Two days later, Brandon once more found himself standing on the stoop before a familiar green door. Only, now a festive wreath, complete with pine cones and not one, but three gold and green ribbons, festooned the panel.

He grinned as he flicked the end of one ribbon, then knocked briskly three times.

Knock. Knock. Knock.

This wreath, like all of the others adorning the house, was another gift from him.

He'd not accepted no for an answer, nor let Mrs. Thackpenny's grumbling and criticisms sway him. With persistence, kindness, and gentleness, he'd gradually persuaded Mrs. Thackpenny to lower her battlements by small increments until the elderly woman was hardly recognizable.

Once she'd shucked her thorny exterior, his patient proved to be keen-witted and possessed a rather wicked sense of humor.

In short, Mrs. Thackpenny was utterly delightful.

Brandon couldn't help but feel the improvement in her temperament had also benefited the others in her household. Whereas before, he was typically met with stern, solemn-faced servants, now they bore smiles.

Just the other day, he'd even caught the much jollier Flannery flirting with Mrs. Wilkie beneath the kissing bough. Color had infused their flushed faces, and a romantic spark shone in their eyes.

Brandon would like to catch Joy beneath that same kissing bough. Today was her birthday, and he'd been invited to dine with her and Mrs. Thackpenny.

When was the last time they'd invited a guest for dinner?

It wouldn't surprise him if his much-improved patient hadn't dined with anyone other than a companion for a decade or more.

He'd not even lowered his hand to his side before the door swung open.

Flannery stood there in a sharp new black suit, appearing as pompous and official as any ducal butler. "Good evening, sir," he drawled with the perfect blend of deference and confidence that only a butler could convey.

"Good evening, Flanders."

Disappointment rutted around Brandon's middle because Joy hadn't answered his summons as she frequently did. But then again, perhaps, she was taking special care with her appearance. It was her birthday, after all. Brandon had broken every societal protocol in having a gown made for the occasion.

Not giving a donkey's behind, he'd stepped way beyond the mark and asked Mrs. Wilkie to procure Joy and Mrs. Thackpenny's measurements. After a bit of cajoling and intentional charming on his part, he'd finally persuaded the woman to do his bidding. Or mayhap, it was the promise of a Christmas goose and all of the trimmings that caused the cook's eventual capitulation.

This afternoon, the gowns had been delivered to Joy and her companion. A soft wild rose for Mrs. Thackpenny, which the knowledgeable modiste had insisted was perfectly appropriate for a mature woman. And for Joy, an ice-blue evening gown trimmed in Mechlin lace to match her remarkable eyes.

Tonight, he planned to invite them to join him for Christmas at Rockford Park. Even Mrs.

Thackpenny's pets were welcome. He'd already sent word to Connor. His older brother had responded in his usual bantering manner, asking if Brandon had, at last, lost his heart.

Yes, big brother, my prayers have been answered. I have fallen in love with the most remarkable, extraordinary, beautiful woman.

However, his brother would not be made privy to that information until the woman who'd possessed Brandon's heart was aware of that fact herself. He had every intention of rectifying that situation at the earliest opportunity.

"Your coat, my lord?" Flannery frequently addressed Brandon by his peerage honorific.

Brandon suspected it was because he was the only lord to grace this house in decades, and it made the aged servant feel important.

Taking in the bouquet of evergreens and holly atop a new table in the entry, he smiled inwardly. The place looked like a home now and not a gloomy mausoleum.

"Thank you, Flannery," Brandon said, passing his outwear to the man. "Are they in the salon?"

"Mrs. Thackpenny is, sir. Miss Winterborne has not come down yet."

After setting Brandon's possessions aside, Flannery drew himself up. He gripped his crisp lapels in either hand and noisily cleared his throat. Staring straight ahead at some point beyond Brandon's shoulder, the servant intoned, "Mrs. Wilkie and I would like to express our appreciation and gratitude for the changes you have wrought in this household, my lord. I never would have believed it possible had I not witnessed the transformation with my own eyes."

Brandon clasped the man's boney shoulder. "All it takes is a little Christmas spirit, persistence, patience, and a generous dose of kindness."

"I don't know about that, my lord, but we are most indebted to you. It seems you are able to heal the soul as well as the body." He inclined his head, his sparse gray hair slicked back with pomade. "This way, if you please."

Checking a smile at the man's formal air, Brandon allowed himself to be guided to the salon.

"Lord Brandon Morrisette," Flannery intoned with the solemnity of a royal majordomo.

The furniture had been rearranged to accommodate a hotter fire. Nonetheless, as was her wont, Mrs. Thackpenny sat upon her usual settee. A queen upon her throne. Poppet on one side and Whiskers on the other. A smile wreathed her lined face. Attired in the gown he'd secretly ordered and had delivered, she lifted her gloved hands to him in welcome.

"Doctor Morrisette."

Ah, so she'd actually worn the gown.

Brandon considered that a huge milestone to have achieved. After five decades, she'd finally put aside her mourning weeds. Hopefully, she would look to her future now rather than dwell in the past.

"My dear boy. You've truly outdone yourself." Mrs. Thackpenny beamed, the pale rose satin giving her skin a healthy glow. She'd even donned a diamond pendant, earrings, and a bracelet. A trace of the once beautiful woman still lingered, and dressed in her finery, she presented quite a regal figure.

"Madam, you are a vision." Brandon bent over her hand.

She blushed and tutted. "Flatterer."

He glanced at the mantel clock then to the empty doorway.

Where was Joy?

Had he offended her by also sending the gown?

It was wildly improper.

Way, way, *way* beyond the pale.

Perhaps Mrs. Thackpenny had refused to allow her to wear it.

No, if that were the case, then the elderly dame would've declined to wear hers as well. Brandon was sure of it.

"She'll be down shortly." Mrs. Thackpenny seemed to have read his mind. "Don't think I haven't noticed the way you two look at each other when you think I'm unaware, Doctor. My eyesight may be failing, but I'd have to be blind to miss the heated exchanges between you."

He resisted the urge to claw at his suddenly too-tight neckcloth.

What did one say to that?

Then she utterly flummoxed him by giving him a conspiratorial wink. "I was young once too."

Feeling like a lad caught with his sticky fingers in the sweet jar, Brandon fell back upon his doctor's charm. "Your company is all that I require, Mrs. Thackpenny."

"Pshaw. Balderdash." She waved a gloved hand at him, the diamonds in her bracelet catching the candlelight and twinkling like stars in the midnight sky. "Do not try to change the subject, scamp."

Aye, Mrs. Thackpenny was too perceptive by far.

Head tilted, she eyed him keenly, a hint of sadness tempering her jesting. "I suspect I may be searching for a new companion soon."

Astute woman.

If Joy agreed to become his wife.

Brandon put a palm to his jacket pocket where a ring box lay securely ensconced. It was both a birthday present and a betrothal ring if all went as planned this evening.

"I shall miss Joy tremendously." A shadow flitted across Mrs. Thackpenny's features, stealing her earlier happiness. Running a gentle hand over each of her pets, she murmured, "She's been unfailingly kind and patient with me when I did not deserve it."

Pride bloomed in his chest, but all he said was, "She is an exceptional woman, to be sure."

He intended to consult with Joy about Mrs. Thackpenny living with them. However, he'd not make that offer to the elderly woman without Joy's input. She had a warm, forgiving nature, but it might be asking too much to have her former employer, a woman who had not been the kindest to her, live with them.

Mrs. Thackpenny glanced up, a distinct sheen of tears behind her spectacle lenses. "I regret wasting so many years harboring bitterness and grief." A long sigh slipped past her lips as she stared beyond him. "The things I might've done. The places I might've visited."

Brandon perched his hips on the edge of the tea table and took her gnarled hands in his. "It's not too late, Mrs. Thackpenny."

"Please do call me Sabella." Blinking rapidly, she squeezed his fingers. "Thank you, Brandon, for all that you have done. May I call you Brandon?"

"Of course."

A nascent smile bent her mouth. "You helped me to see the good in the world again. To have hope and to forgive God for taking my dearest Ephraim from me. Joy did as well. In truth, my fear of losing her made me keep her at arm's length. I couldn't bear to lose someone else I loved. I've come to love her like a daughter, you see."

"Good evening." Joy's melodious voice floated into the room, even as she drifted to the center of the parlor.

Rendered speechless, Brandon gaped.

By Jove, she was an absolute vision.

She'd piled her hair atop her head into a

chignon, leaving a few fiery silky curls to trail over one shoulder. The gown fit her to perfection, emphasizing her womanly charms and making her eyes glitter like the very stars in the sky. She wore a sapphire and pearl parure set, no doubt loaned from Sabella.

"Oh, my dear girl," breathed Sabella, her eyes misty and proud. "You are absolutely stunning." She poked Brandon with her ever-present cane. "*Well?* What are you waiting for? Get on with it."

Yes, Sabella Thackpenny had changed significantly. However, Brandon suspected she'd always be a bit crusty and outspoken. In truth, he admired her spunk.

His heart kicking against his ribcage, he rose and went to Joy. He raised her hand to his mouth and then dared to kiss her fingertips. Even through her satin gloves, her heat beckoned, and a frisson sluiced through him.

"You take my breath away, Joy."

Eyes shining, she looked him up and down. "The same might be said of you, Doctor."

"Thank you for wearing the gown."

Never have I beheld a more entrancing woman.

Her smile widened, revealing her unrestrained happiness. "Thank you for gifting me it."

If Sabella Thackpenny weren't sitting a few feet away, nothing on earth would've kept Brandon from sweeping Joy into his arms and kissing her breathless. When she looked at him like that, her eyes soft and worshipful, like he was her hero, a chivalrous knight of old, and she'd follow him to the ends of the earth, he wanted to ask her to be his wife right then and there.

Hold on, old boy. Later, when you can do the thing properly.

Tucking her hand into the crook of his elbow, he turned them to face Sabella. "I'd like to invite you both to join my family at Rockford Park for the holiday."

~*~

Sabella's eyes rounded, and her jaw went slack before she dropped her attention first to Whiskers and then Poppet. Slowly, she raised an uncertain gaze to Brandon's, a silent question in their depths.

He quirked his mouth to the side. "Of course, your pets are welcome too."

'That's very generous of you," Joy put in smoothly, eyeing her confounded employer. "However, I'm not certain it would be proper for me to attend."

"Proper? *Proper?*" Sabella's biting inflection was back in place.

As if to protect her from her employer's displeasure, Brandon drew Joy nearer.

Clutching her cane, Sabella slowly levered to her feet. Both hands clasping the grip, she leaned heavily upon the support. "Gel, we're wearing gowns Brandon had made for us. He's bestowed dozens of gifts upon us. He's also been seen entering this house and strolling The Vines for days now." She chuckled, the raspy sound like old paper crinkling. "We are *way* beyond proper, and I, for one, relish it."

Thump. Thump.

"I…" Puzzling her brow, Joy looked up at Brandon. "She has a point, but I cannot help but feel that your family and others will make inaccurate assumptions. It could prove awkward for you, Brandon."

"Hmph, *not* if he asks you to marry him," Sabella said matter-of-factly, as she tottered toward the doorway, Whiskers and Poppet trailing her. "As his betrothed, no one would raise an eyebrow. I plan on attending, Joy dear. In truth, I am quite looking forward to the festivities. However, I shan't force you to accompany me."

"I should like to attend, as well." Joy glanced

at Brandon, her heart stuttering at his exuberant grin of approval.

Sabella paused on the threshold and half-turned toward them.

"By the by, Joy, dear. I've not said anything before, but I think it bears mentioning, for it is quite obvious to anyone with eyes in their heads." She shot Brandon a speaking glance. "Your resemblance to Lady Joanna, the deceased Countess of Winterbanks, is nothing short of remarkable. Someone else might make the connection as well."

Eyes shining with an unmistakable glint, the merest hint of a smile touched her thin lips.

Precious Lord.

Lungs cramping from shock, Joy dug her fingertips into Brandon's arm. She strove to remain composed, her mind honing in on one critical point.

She knows.

She knows that I'm a bastard.

How?

And how long has she been privy to that knowledge?

Joy swallowed, unable to form a response. No, unable to speak due to her heart having launched itself into her throat, where it remained lodged and beating a panicked cadence.

And she suspects she knows who my mother is—was.

A wholly unforeseen wave of sadness poured over Joy. She'd never entertained any notion of finding her parents. But if the countess was indeed her mother, she'd never have a chance to meet her.

You wouldn't have anyway, in all likelihood.

"In case you are concerned that I'll sack you, Joy, I don't give a beggar's prayer about your parentage." A kind smile wreathed Sabella's face. "I've suspected since the day I retained you as my companion that you might claim an unacknowledged relationship to the former countess. You needn't fear it makes a jot of difference to me."

Such relief winged through Joy, she almost sagged against Brandon. "That's very kind of you."

"Now, I'll leave you two alone." Sabella lifted her cane and gestured between Brandon and Joy. "Do get on with it, though, Brandon. I'm quite famished, and we're having *Coq au Vin*." She flashed a girlish grin. "Mrs. Wilkie has been experimenting in the kitchen. I find I quite anticipate what she'll next prepare."

With that proclamation, she departed, leaving Brandon and Joy gaping after her.

8

Shaking his head, Brandon stared at the empty doorway.

Sabella's bold as brass intimations that he should propose at once were overshadowed by that peculiar comment about the countess. Given Joy's sudden pallor and the conflicting emotions rapidly parading across her face, he'd wager she knew what Sabella's remarks meant.

"Joy?" He turned her to face him and notched her chin upward with a finger until she reluctantly met his gaze. "Are you all right?"

His much-anticipated proposal would have to

wait.

Face taut, she blinked several times, her lashes sweeping slowly up and down, almost as if she didn't see him.

"What is it, sweetheart?" Brandon cupped her cheek, brushing his thumb over the incredible softness.

Her gaze riveted on his before skittering away.

"Brandon, I must tell you something."

"You know you can tell me anything, my darling." Smiling, he kissed her forehead. Now that he could finally claim her as his, once he declared himself, that was, he couldn't seem to stop kissing her. "Is it something we should sit down for?"

Head angled, she considered that for a moment, then gave a little nod. "Yes, I believe so."

"Then sit, we shall." He took her hand and led her to one of the other settees. After seeing her settled, he sat beside her and took her hand in his once more. "Tell me. What has you troubled?"

"I've been a companion to Mrs. Thackpenny for five years." Joy's shoulders rose, and her bosom expanded as she drew in a deep breath. "This has been my first and only position."

Brandon knew that already, but he wouldn't rush her explanation.

"I was raised in a foundling home called Haven House and Academy for the Enrichment of Young Women," she said.

She fidgeted with the edge of a small, hideously ugly needlepoint pillow squished between her and the side of the settee. Reciting the tale as if she'd rehearsed it many times, she swiftly explained how all of the girls from Haven House and Academy for the Enrichment of Young Women were illegitimate daughters of desire. All were born on the wrong side of the blanket.

Raising her chin, which quivered the merest bit, she bravely forged onward. "I'll understand if you want nothing further to do with me, now that you know my shameful secret."

"Silly, foolish darling," he murmured low, his voice tight with emotion.

As if the circumstances of her birth would in any way diminish his love for her.

Joy jutted her chin out, and no poker was straighter or stiffer than her rigid spine. "You think my being a bastard is *silly*? That my concerns are foolish?" she accused, hurt leaking into her clipped words.

"Shh," he soothed, trailing his fingertips over her forearm. "Don't take umbrage, sweet, for I meant no offense."

Brandon drew her stiff form into his arms and kissed those silky red-gold curls. She smelled divine. He inhaled her lemon essence deep into his lungs as he gently caressed the tension from her back.

At last, she relaxed against him, burrowing her face into his chest.

"I don't give a fig about your past or your paternity, Joy. All that matters is that you agree to spend the future with me as my wife."

She tilted her head upward, her blue, blue eyes searching his.

"How can you say that? My shame will taint you. You're a doctor, Brandon. The son of a marquess. Your patients and your family—"

"Have absolutely no say in who I love or who I want to spend the rest of my life with." He brushed his lips over hers, nearly groaning at their sweet, sweet softness. A hint of mint and tea lingered, and he couldn't help but wonder if she'd sipped mint tea before coming below.

To soothe her nerves?

"And I choose you, Joy...Winterborne." Grinning, he said, "I don't know your middle name."

"I have three, actually," she said softly, her expression slightly dazed. As if she couldn't quite believe Brandon truly wished to make her his wife. "Shepard, Natalia, and Martha." She tipped her mouth into a winsome smile. "All of the girls from Haven House and Academy for the Enrichment of Young Women share the middle name Shepard."

"Ah, after Mrs. Hester Shepherd?"

Joy nodded. "She has no children of her own."

"Well, I choose you, Joy Shephard Natalia Martha Winterborne, to be my wife." He stole another kiss from her irresistible rosebud mouth.

"Forever." Kiss.

"And always." Kiss.

Joy's eyes grew misty, and a tremulous smile curved her mouth. "You truly love me?"

He gave a solemn nod, somehow knowing

this wasn't the time to jest or tease. She doubted his sincerity and needed reassurance that she, and only she, would ever be Mrs. Brandon Morrisette.

"I do, my lady. My heart. My love."

Giving a watery chuckle, she entwined her arms around his neck. "I'm not a lady, even if my mother *was* the Countess of Winterbanks. A claim, which I'm sure I'll never know the truth of."

Angling so that his spine rested against the settee's worn fabric, Brandon swept Joy onto his lap.

A tiny yelp rent the air, but she giggled and tightened her grip around his neck. Pressing his mouth to first one cheek and then the other, he managed between kisses, "You'll be a lady as my wife."

"A lady?" She scrunched her adorable nose. "I never thought to marry, let alone become a lady. What will your family say?"

"That I am a very, *very* lucky man."

Her mouth sweeping upward, she gave the slightest nod.

"Does that mean you will marry me, Joy?" Brandon framed her chin between his forefinger and thumb. "I've loved you for so very long. I think since the first time you opened that godawful green front door and the sun burst from *inside* the house, blinding me.

"You, sir, are waxing poetic." A radiant smile arced her mouth. "I confess, I do like it. Very much."

She nestled further into his lap.

Zounds, she'd kill him if she kept squirming like that.

He gave a little growl and nipped Joy's earlobe.

She half-sighed, half-moaned, arching her neck to allow him full access to the ivory column.

He nibbled his way along the milky white skin, softer than the finest silk.

"You haven't answered me, my love," Brandon murmured against that satiny flesh.

Her lashes fluttered open, and a siren's smile curled the corners of her pretty mouth. "I find I cannot concentrate when you're kissing me."

With a reluctant sigh, he set her from him. He'd never finish this proposal business with her seated on his lap.

Her passion-heavy gaze nearly undid him.

After fishing around in his pocket, Brandon removed the box hidden there and opened the lid. A narrow band, studded with diamonds and emeralds, glittered within a white satin nest.

"Happy birthday, darling."

"Oh, Brandon." Joy gasped, pressing one hand to her throat.

Sliding from the settee, he took one knee before her. "Marry me, Joy. Let us grow old together. Share life's joys and sorrows in each other's arms. I love you, and—"

"Yes. Yes." She threw her arms around his neck, raining kisses over his jaw and chin and cheeks. "Yes. I'll marry you." Her blue eyes shining, she drew a few inches away. "I was already half in love with you. But that day you examined Sir Galahad Whiskerton and Lady Persephone Poppington, my heart became irrevocably yours."

He chuckled at the memory. "Let's not have a long betrothal. I've waited an entire lifetime for you."

Brandon slid the ring on her finger.

Joy bit her lower lip. "I would like to marry straight away, but what about Mrs. Thackpenny?" She dashed a swift glance toward the doorway. "I cannot just leave her, Brandon. She's become my family, and I care deeply about her."

"I wanted to discuss that with you." He grinned as he stood and pulled Joy to her feet as well. "How would you feel about her living with us?"

"Are you sure?" Joy's eyes went impossibly wide with excitement and hope. "As you know, she doesn't have the easiest of temperaments."

"I'm agreeable if she is," Brandon said with a shrug.

A commotion carried to them from outside the door moments before Sabella's uneven, shuffling gate accompanied by the *clump, clump* of her cane announced her presence. Sniffling loudly, she managed through her soft weeping. "*She* is most agreeable."

Brandon chuckled, not at all surprised to learn she'd been earwigging on their conversation. "Then, I'll procure a special license, and we'll marry over the Christmastide holiday."

He opened his arms, and Joy stepped into his embrace.

"My Christmas wish came early," she said, blinking away the crystalline droplets of happiness.

Brandon cocked an eyebrow. "And what, may I ask, did you wish for?"

"You, Brandon. *You* were my Christmas wish."

Epilogue

25 December 1817

Rockford House

Lying on her side, Joy watched her husband of five days sleep, his breathing deep and steady. Dark blond stubble shadowed his rugged jawline. A little shudder rippled through her as she recalled how that light beard felt against her bare skin.

Lord, how she loved him.

Less than a month ago, she'd been bemoaning her fate, dreading what her future held, and now, she was a lady, married to the most marvelous of men.

Brandon stirred, and reaching out, drew her into his strong embrace. Cracking an eyelid open, he gave her one of his bone-melting, seductive smiles.

"I caught you," he said, his voice husky from sleep.

Yes, she liked to watch him sleep—this man who was hers for all time.

"What do you intend to do about it?" she asked, her voice suddenly sultry with awareness.

With a throaty growl, he nipped her neck.

Much later, when Joy was nestled in his arms and his breath warmed her scalp, Joy whispered against his chest, "I love you, Brandon."

"And I you, my darling wife." He edged her chin upward with his forefinger. "Happy Christmas. Thank you for giving me the most precious gift I'll ever receive."

As his breathing slowed and fell into the even rhythm she'd come to recognize when he slept, Joy smiled and snuggled closer.

When she was old and gray, she'd tell her grandchildren and their children to be sure to make a Christmas wish.

You never know when one will come true.

About the Author

USA Today Bestselling, award-winning author COLLETTE CAMERON® scribbles Scottish and Regency historical romance novels featuring dashing rogues, rakes, and scoundrels and the strong heroines who reform them. Blessed with an overactive and witty muse that won't stop whispering new romantic romps in her ear, she's lived in Oregon her entire life. Although she dreams of living in Scotland part-time. A confessed Cadbury chocoholic, you'll always find a dash of inspiration and a pinch of humor in her sweet-to-spicy timeless romances®.

Explore **Collette's worlds** at collettecameron.com!

Join her **VIP Reader Club** and **FREE newsletter**.

Giggles guaranteed!

FREE BOOK: Join Collette's The Regency Rose®
VIP Reader Club to get updates on book releases,
cover reveals, contests and giveaways she reserves
exclusively for email and newsletter followers. Also,
any deals, sales, or special promotions are offered to
club members first. She will not share your name or
email, nor will she spam you.

http://bit.ly/TheRegencyRoseGift

Dearest Reader,

Thank you for reading A LADY, A KISS, A CHRISTMAS WISH. This Christmas novella launches my Daughters of Desire (Scandalous Ladies) series. I've been so excited to start this series, which features illegitimate heroines.

As I'm sure you are aware, respectable employment opportunities for women were severely limited during the Regency era. However, the women who are raised at Haven House are also guaranteed training in the profession of their choice. You see, though the girls are cast-offs, at least one of their parents cared enough to ensure them a place in the extremely exclusive orphanage.

To stay abreast of the releases of the books in

series, you can subscribe to my newsletter (the link is below) or visit my author world at collettecameron.com. I hope Brandon and Joy's romance brought a little Christmas spirit into your life and provided you with a pleasant escape for a little while.

Hugs,

Collette

Connect with Collette!

collettecameron.com

NO LADY FOR THE LORD

Daughters of Desire (Scandalous Ladies), Book Two

She was only supposed to care for his wards…
not fall in love with him.

He was a carefree rogue…

Lord Ronan Brockman had a perfect life. Handsome, wealthy, and beholden to no one, he was charmed. But that was before he was unexpectedly named guardian to two young girls—and before he met their fascinating governess. Acting on his attraction to the witty beauty would be utter madness. Unfortunately, that doesn't seem to be enough to dissuade him from pursuing her…

She can never let her guard down…

Mercy Feathers knows more about responsibility than a rogue like Ronan could ever fathom. But to her *great* consternation, despite his *many* flaws, she wants him with an all-consuming passion that's as shocking as it is forbidden. It's just her misfortune that there's only one way a relationship with him could end—and it *isn't* with happily ever after…

Is their love enough?

Can Ronan and Mercy overcome all that stands between them—including the ghosts of her past—and take a shot at true love? Only if they're willing to open their hearts and break a few rules…

Made in the USA
Middletown, DE
08 December 2022

17628225R00086